Written by Sue Graves
Illustrated by Alison Atkins (John Martin & Artists)
Designed by Blue Sunflower Creative

Language consultant: Betty Root

This is a Parragon Publishing book
This edition published in 2004

Parragon Publishing
Queen Street House
4 Queen Street
Bath, BA1 1HE, UK

ISBN 1-40541-858-3
Printed in China

Noisy Train

p

Notes for Parents

Reading with your child is an
enjoyable and rewarding experience.
These **Gold Stars** reading books
encourage and support children
who are learning to read.

The **Gold Stars** reading books are filled with fun stories, familiar vocabulary, and amusing pictures. Sharing these books with your child will ensure that reading is fun. It is important, at this early stage, for children to enjoy reading and succeed. Success creates confidence.

Starting to read

Start by reading the book aloud to your child, taking time to talk about the pictures. This will help your child to see that pictures often give clues about the story.

Over a period of time, try to read the same book several times so that your child becomes familiar with the story and the words and phrases. Gradually your child will want to read the book aloud with you. It helps to run your finger under the words as you say them.

Occasionally, stop and encourage your child to continue reading aloud without you. Join in again when your child needs help. This is the next step toward helping your child become an independent reader.

Finally, your child will be ready to read alone. Listen carefully to your child and give plenty of praise. Remember to make reading an enjoyable experience.

Using your Gold Stars stickers

You can use the **Gold Stars** stickers at the back of the book as a reward for effort as well as achievement. Learning to read is an exciting challenge for every child.

Remember these four important stages:

- Read the story **to** your child.
- Read the story **with** your child.
- Encourage your child to read **to you**.
- Listen to your child read **alone**.

This is Noisy Train.
Noisy Train is very noisy.

He likes to blow his whistle.
"Toot, toot!"

He likes to blow it very loudly!

Every day, Noisy Train
saw Sheep.

"Toot, toot!" said Noisy Train.
"Hello, Sheep!"

Every day, Sheep got annoyed.

"Baa, baa!" said Sheep.
"What a noisy train!"

Every day, Noisy Train saw
Sheepdog.

"Toot, toot!" said Noisy Train.
"Hello, Sheepdog!"

Every day, Sheepdog got
annoyed.

"Woof, woof!" said Sheepdog.
"What a noisy train!"

Sheep and Sheepdog went to
see Noisy Train.

"You are too noisy," they said.
"Stop blowing your whistle."

Noisy Train was sad.

"I'll stop blowing my whistle," he said.

The next day, Noisy Train saw Sheep, but he didn't blow his whistle.

Baa, baa!

Sheep was pleased.

"Baa, baa!" she said.
"That's better."

Then, Noisy Train saw
Sheepdog, but he didn't blow
his whistle.

Sheepdog was pleased.

"Woof, woof!" he said.
"That's better."

But then, Noisy Train saw the lambs.

The lambs were on the track.

"The lambs must be moved,"
said Noisy Train. "I must get
Sheep and Sheepdog."

Noisy Train flashed his lights.
"Flash, flash!"

Flash, flash!

He puffed out steam.
"Puff, puff!"

But Sheep and Sheepdog did
not come.

"I will have to blow my whistle," said Noisy Train. "Then Sheep and Sheepdog will come."

Toot, toot!

Noisy Train blew his whistle.
"Toot, toot!" He blew it very
loudly.

Sheep and Sheepdog came
running. They got the lambs
to move off the track.

"Baa, baa!" said Sheep. "Woof, woof!" said Sheepdog. "We're glad you are a noisy train!"

Read these words. Look back in the book and find the words.

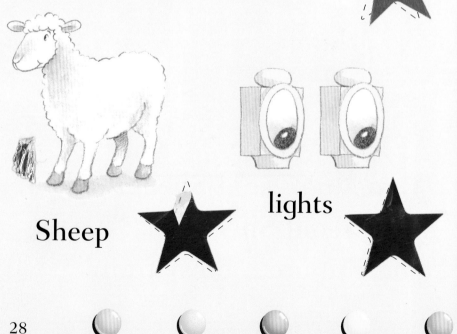

Noisy Train

Sheep

lights

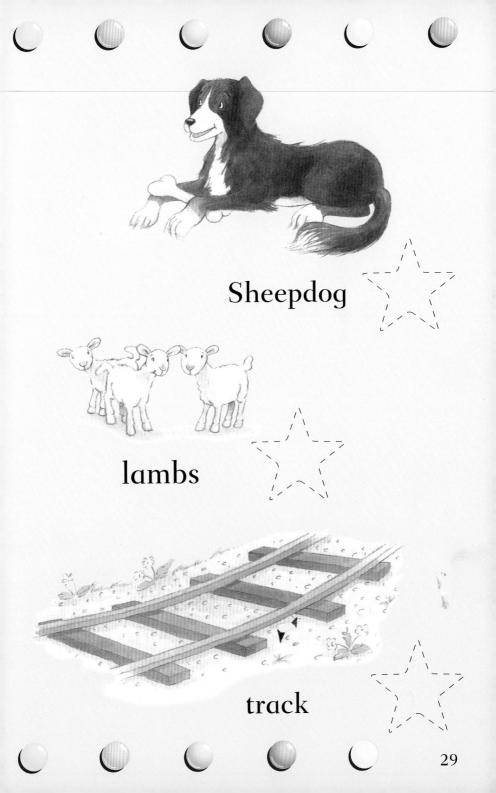

Sheepdog

lambs

track

Gold Stars reading books are for children who are beginning to read.

- Familiar, repeated vocabulary
- Short sentences
- Large, clear type
- Pictures that support the text
- Review activity